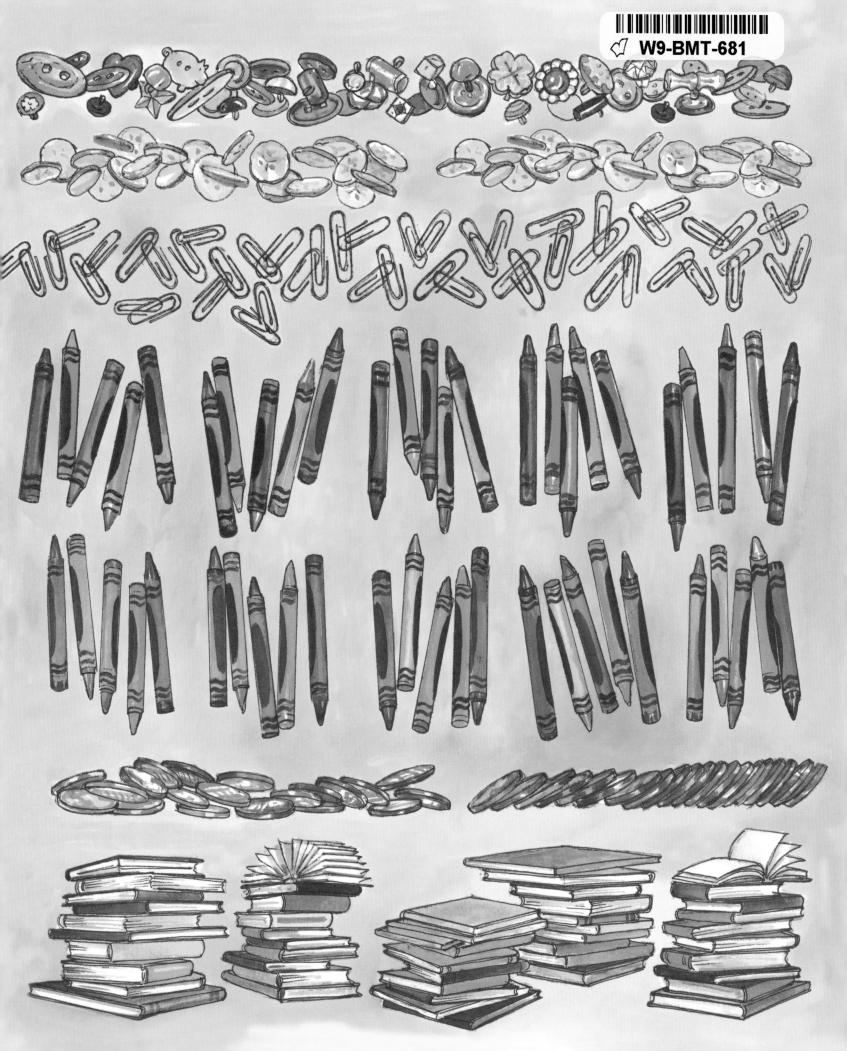

Jake's
100th Day
of School

This book is dedicated to the most extraordinary principal I have ever met,
Dr. Reba M. Wadsworth,
who puts children first every day, in every way.

And for Chase,
who forgot his project and sparked the fuel of my imagination.

—L. L. L.

To my wonderful extended family who have loved,
supported, and cheered me on throughout my life.
And a big thank-you to the Daniel Butler and Winn Brook Elementary Schools
for inviting me to share their 100th Day celebrations.

—J. L.

Ω

Published by
PEACHTREE PUBLISHERS
1700 Chattahoochee Avenue
Atlanta, Georgia 30318-2112

www.peachtree-online.com

Text © 2006 by Lester L. Laminack
Illustrations © 2006 by Judy Love

First trade paperback edition published in 2008

Book design by Loraine M. Joyner
Typesetting by Melanie McMahon Ives

Illustrations created with pencil, ink, and watercolor on 100% rag hot press watercolor
paper. Titles typeset in Chalkboard, bylines typeset in Zemke Hand ITC, text typeset
in Goudy Infant.

Printed and manufactured in Singapore
10 9 8 7 6 5 4 (hardcover)
10 9 8 7 6 5 4 3 2 1 (trade paperback)

Library of Congress Cataloging-in-Publication Data
Laminack, Lester L., 1956-
  Jake's 100th day of school / Lester L. Laminack ; illustrated by Judy
Love. -- 1st ed.
    p. cm.
  Summary: Jake is so excited about his 100th Day of School, he runs
to catch the school bus without his project, but fortunately, with the
help of his principal, Jake is able to find a perfect substitute for his
project.
  ISBN 13: 978-1-56145-355-9 / ISBN 10: 1-56145-355-2 (hardcover)
  ISBN 13: 978-1-56145-463-1 / ISBN 10: 1-56145-463-X (trade paperback)
  [1. Hundredth Day of School--Fiction. 2. Schools--Fiction. 3. Show-
and-tell presentations--Fiction.]   I. Love, Judith DuFour, ill. II. Title.
III. Title: Jake's one hundredth day of school. IV. Title: Jake's
hundredth day of school.
PZ7.L1815Jak 2006
[E]--dc22
                            2005020882

Jake's 100th Day of School

LESTER L. LAMINACK

Illustrations by
JUDY LOVE

PEACHTREE
ATLANTA

Mr. Thompson's class was excited. Tomorrow would be the 100th day of school.

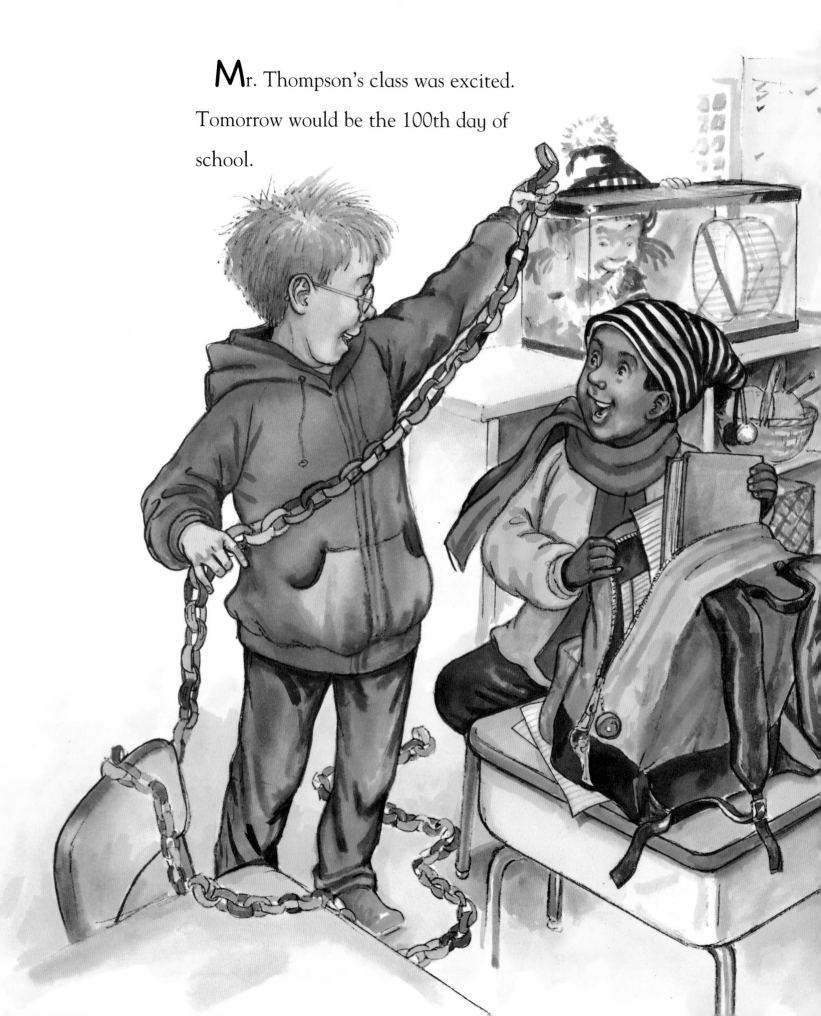

Every day since school began, Mr. Thompson started class by adding one link to the Good Morning Chain. Tomorrow they would add the 100th link, and all the students would bring their collections of 100 things.

Mr. Thompson said he had a *superrific* surprise planned, too—a visit from Jake's Grandma Maggie. Everyone knew that meant something wonderful would happen.

Mr. Thompson was in the classroom very early on the 100th day. He wanted to have everything ready for the big event. "Yep," he said to himself, "today is the big day!"

Jake was so excited about the 100th day that he rushed out the door to catch the school bus...
But he left something very important at home.

He didn't even think about his book bag until the bus stopped for Emily. When he saw her wearing a chain of paper clips around her neck, Jake felt a flutter in his stomach.

When he saw Henry boarding the bus with 100 bottle caps glued on a poster, Jake felt a lump in his throat.

When Douglas showed his collection of 100 signatures, big tears welled up in Jake's eyes.

By the time Jake arrived at school, he was surrounded

by hundreds and hundreds of things.

A hundred buttons.

A hundred marbles.

A hundred rubber bands.

And sailing all around his head,

a hundred paper planes...

A hundred cookies.

A hundred pencils.

A hundred beads in braids.

And hanging from a wooden rod,

a hundred lucky cranes...

Hundreds and

hundreds and

hundreds of things.

"Good morning, Jake," said Mrs. Wadsworth, the principal. "Are you all set for the 100th day of school?"

Jake stood like a statue and looked at her. He couldn't make a word come out of his mouth. He couldn't stop the tears spilling from his eyes.

"Did you forget?" Mrs. Wadsworth asked. Her voice was softer than a pillow. Jake could only nod his head. Mrs. Wadsworth put her arm around his shoulders. "Come in my office. We'll think of something."

EXTENSION

Jake climbed into the big chair and Mrs. Wadsworth sat next to him. "Could we call someone at home to bring your collection?" she asked.

"Everyone's at work," Jake said, sniffling. "Grandma Maggie's not home either. She's getting ready for the *superrific* surprise."

"Let's check around here," said Mrs. Wadsworth. "I'll bet we can find a hundred of something."

"I don't know," Jake said, "a hundred is a whole lot of stuff."

"Do you suppose I have a hundred paper clips in this jar?" she asked, lifting it for him to see.

"It doesn't look like a hundred," Jake said. "Besides, Emily is wearing a hundred paper clips." He looked around the office.

"Mrs. Wadsworth, all you've got in your office is books—lots and lots of books. I guess we could make a collection of books."

"Absolutely, Jake," Mrs. Wadsworth said with a smile. "One hundred books would make a wonderful collection for a super reader like you. Let's see if I have that many."

Jake and Mrs. Wadsworth took books from her shelves. They counted ten books and made a stack, ten more and ten more until they had ten stacks. Jake touched each stack as he carefully counted them: 10, 20, 30, 40, 50, 60, 70, 80, 90, 100.

"Wow, Mrs. Wadsworth. That's 100 books!"

Together they rolled the cart of books down the hallway to Room 24. Jake added his collection to all the others.

Then he made a sign:

100 Books
from
Mrs. Wadsworth's
Office

When all the projects were on display, Mr. Thompson told the class that it was time to begin the 100th day of school. "Mrs. Wadsworth," he said, "before you go back to your office would you add the 100th link to the Good Morning Chain?"

The morning was filled with even more hundreds. The 100th check was marked on the I Fed Goldilocks Chart. The 100th knot was tied on the Days of Reading Rope. And some kids took turns sharing their collections of 100 things.

Then around ten o'clock, there was a knock at the door. When Mr. Thompson opened it, Jake's Grandma Maggie came in with someone the kids had never seen. The surprise visitor walked with a wooden stick, stepping very slowly into the room.

"Good morning, boys and girls," Grandma Maggie said. "This is my Aunt Lula. Can anyone guess why I brought my Aunt Lula for the 100th day of school?"

"Maybe it's 'cause of that stick," Henry said. "I'll bet there's 100 ribbons on it."

Aunt Lula eased into Mr. Thompson's chair and chuckled. "Well, you are a very clever boy," she said. "I did tie 100 ribbons on my walking stick."

"But that's not the only reason," said Grandma Maggie. "My Aunt Lula is 100 years old."

"Wow!" was all the children could say, and the sound of it swooshed across the room like wind on the playground.

"Aunt Lula and I are going to help you make a special snack," Grandma Maggie said, unrolling a chart with their recipe written on it.

After all the kids finished their 100th day snack, they sat together to hear about more projects.

Jake was the last to share his 100th day project. "I made a picture book of 100 memories, except I forgot it this morning," he said. "But that's okay 'cause Mrs. Wadsworth helped me make a collection of books from her office. She must have a thousand of them in there! I put them in ten stacks of ten, and if you count by tens, that's 100 books."

"Jake, that's an excellent collection," said Mr. Thompson. "I know you also worked very hard on your book of 100 memories. Would you like to bring it in tomorrow? We'd love to see it."

"It wouldn't be the same, Mr. Thompson. Tomorrow will be *101* days of school."

"You're right about that," Jake's teacher said, nodding.

Jake sat thinking for a moment. He looked at Grandma Maggie with a twinkle in his eyes and then he whispered something to Mr. Thompson.

"Good idea, Jake!" said his teacher.

"Grandma Maggie, would you please stand with Aunt Lula near the book cart?" Jake said as he headed out the door. "I'll be right back."

When Jake returned to the classroom with Mrs. Wadsworth, Aunt Lula said, "Alright now, let's show 'em some teeth!"

And Mr. Thompson snapped their picture.

The next day, Jake brought his picture book of 100 memories

to share with the class. But, it wasn't the *100th* day anymore.

Now it was the 101st day and that meant

one more page...

...and a picture everyone remembered.